Time to Sleep

Jill McDougall
Illustrated by James Hart

Contents

How Do You Sleep?

It is time to sleep.
How do you sleep?

Do you sleep on one leg?
No, but some animals do.

Do you sleep in a tree?
No, but some animals do.

Animals sleep in all sorts of ways!

Upside Down

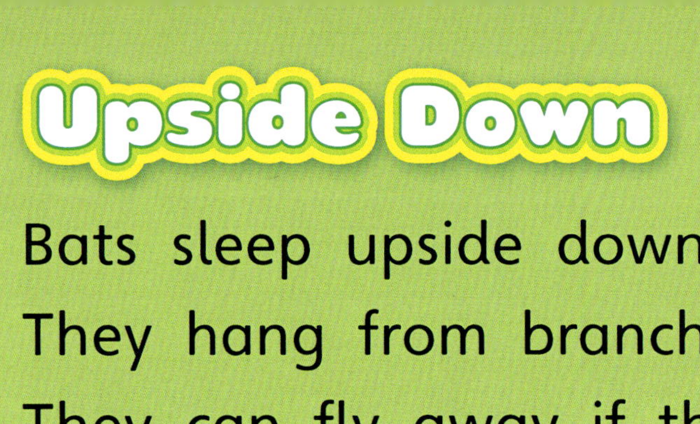

Bats sleep upside down.
They hang from branches by their feet.
They can fly away if they are scared.

Could you sleep upside down?

Standing Up

Horses can sleep standing up.
They lock their legs so they do not fall over.
They can run away if they are scared.

Z Z Z
Could you sleep standing up?

Dolphins sleep with one eye open.
They can see where they are going while they are sleeping.
They can look out for danger.

Could you sleep
with one eye open?

On One Leg

Ducks sleep on one leg.
They tuck the other leg under their feathers.
Then they change legs.
One duck looks out for danger.

Could you sleep
on one leg?

In a Tree

Koalas sleep in trees.
They sleep for most of the day.
They feel safe when they are up high.

Could you sleep
in a tree?

Anywhere!

Cats like to sleep a lot.
They sleep in all sorts of ways.
They sleep in all sorts of places!

If *you* could sleep anywhere, where would you sleep?

Picture Index